Danny's Crazy Christmas

•BRIANÓG BRADY DAWSON•

Pictures by Michael Connor

THE O'BRIEN PRESS
DUBLIN

First published 2008 by The O'Brien Press Ltd,
12 Terenure Road East, Rathgar, Dublin 6, Ireland.
Tel: +353 1 4923333; Fax: +353 1 4922777
E-mail: books@obrien.ie
Website: www.obrien.ie

 ISBN: 978-1-84717-124-5

British Library Cataloguing-in-Publication Data
Dawson, Brianog Brady
Danny's Crazy Christmas. - (O'Brien pandas ; 37)
1. Christmas stories 2. Children's stories
I. Title II. Connor, Michael
823.9'2[J]

The O'Brien Press receives assistance from

1 2 3 4 5 6 7 8 9 10
08 09 10 11 12 13 14 15

Typesetting, layout, editing, design: The O'Brien Press Ltd
Printed and bound in the UK by CPI Group

PANDA books are for young readers
making their own way
through books.

O'BRIEN SERIES FOR YOUNG READERS

O'BRIEN pandas

O'BRIEN panda legends

O'BRIEN flyers

For all the children in Holy Trinity NS Leopardstown

Can YOU spot the panda hidden in the story?

'Yippee!' said Danny.
He zoomed into
the sitting room.
He jumped over
a big box of decorations.

'Tomorrow is **Christmas**!'
he shouted.

Dad took the box.
'Out of my way, Danny,'
he said.
'I can't find the angel
for the Christmas tree.'

Danny threw some tinsel
on his little sister Susie.
She looked silly.
'Put Susie on top of the tree,
Dad!' he shouted.

Dad switched on the tree lights.
'Go and help Granny
and Mum, Danny,' he said.

ny dashed out
the kitchen.
Granny was busy too.
The kitchen table
was full of clothes.

Danny counted:
three jumpers,
four ties,
two pairs of slippers,
five pairs of gloves,
a big blue dressing gown
and lots and lots of scarves.

'Are you packing, Granny?' he said. 'Are you going somewhere very, very cold?'

Granny got a roll
of fancy paper.
She got some sticky tape.

'Don't be silly, Danny,'
she said.
'I'm wrapping
Christmas presents.'

Danny laughed.

'I'm not silly!' he said.

'You're silly, Granny.

Clothes aren't **presents**!'

Granny began counting
on her fingers.
'Bessie, Tom, Lucy, Ben.'

'And Jill and Rick,' said Mum.
'Don't forget them.
Everybody is coming here
for Christmas.'

'Oh dear!' Granny said.
'I need to buy more presents.'

Mum got her coat.
She got Granny's coat.
She got Danny's coat.

But Danny stamped his foot.
'I'm not going shopping again,' he said crossly.
'I hate the shops.'

Mum was in a hurry.
'Santa's grotto is at the shops,'
she said.
'You can tell him
what you want for Christmas.'

Danny pulled his coat on.
'Hurry up, Granny!' he yelled.
He raced out the door.

'We have to tell Santa
to bring me the
HD Mega Game-Station 4.
My friend Mark says
it's the best!'

The shopping centre
was very noisy and crowded.
Granny got more presents.
Mum got a headache.
Danny got cross.

Then Danny saw a big sign.
'SANTA'S GROTTO!' he read.
He dashed inside.

Santa had a long white beard.
He had a bright red suit.
He had a big friendly smile.

Danny told him what he
wanted for Christmas.

'Oooh!' said Santa.
'That's a **big present**,
Danny! Make sure
there's plenty of room
under your Christmas tree.'

Danny nodded.

Then Santa frowned.
'I hope your **chimney**
is clean, Danny,' he said.
'Dirty chimneys
make my suit very messy.
Mrs Claus gets very cross.'

Danny nodded again.

'One more thing,' said Santa.
'Rudolph gets very hungry.
Put out some **food** for him,
will you?'

Danny nodded again.
I'm going to be very busy,
he thought.

On the way home
they stopped at the
supermarket.

'We need turkey, ham,
brussels sprouts,' Mum said.
Danny thought of Rudolph.
'And lots of carrots,' he said.

When they got home,
Danny put all the carrots
in Mum's roasting tin.
He put the tin
outside the front door.

Rudolph will find them there,
he thought.

Then Danny went to
the Christmas tree.
Dad had left a mess under it.
Danny pushed away
all the empty boxes.

Then he saw Susie
under the tree.
She was eating some tinsel.

'Out of the way, Susie!'
shouted Danny.
'Santa said to leave
plenty of room
under the tree
for **my** Christmas present.'

But Susie didn't move.
So Danny grabbed her legs
and pulled her
away from the tree.

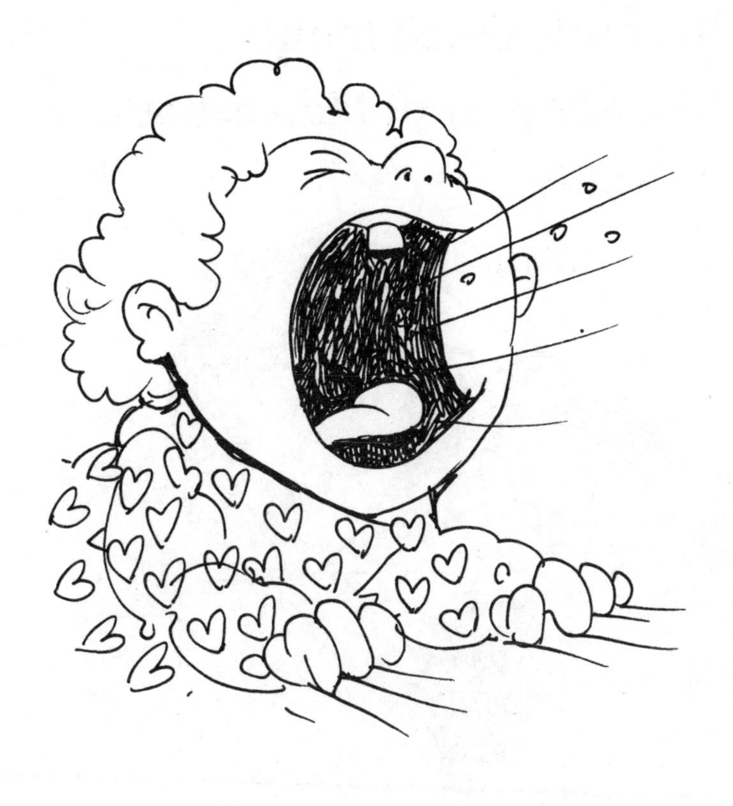

‘**WAAAAAAAA**!’

cried Susie.

‘**WAAAAAAAAAAAAAAA**!’

'Danny!' yelled Mum.
'Go and play at Mark's house.'

Danny made a face at Susie
and ran next door
to Mark's house.

There was a big yellow skip
outside Mark's house.

Danny jumped up
and peeped in.
He saw bits of carpet.
He saw a toaster.
He saw a broken stool.

'Mum cleaned the whole house,' said Mark.
'She dumped lots of rubbish.'

Mark's mum saw them.
'Keep away from that skip, you two!' she yelled.
So Mark and Danny ran back to Danny's house.

They found Granny
in the sitting room.
She was fast asleep.

Danny looked under the tree.
'Oh no,' he said. 'Granny has
put all her presents here.
There's no room
for **my** present.'

He kicked Granny's presents.
'**Stupid clothes presents**!' he said.

'Yuck!' said Mark.
'I hate clothes presents.'
'Yeah!' agreed Danny.
'Clothes are **rubbish**!'

And just then
Danny had a wonderful idea.

He looked at Granny
asleep in the chair.
'Mark, let's dump this rubbish!'
he said. 'Let's put it
in the skip!'

Mark nodded.
'We must be quick,' he said.
'Mum says the men
will take the skip away soon.'

Danny picked up a present.
It had a **big blue ribbon** on it.
'This must be the
stupid dressing gown,'
he said.

He made a face at Granny.

Then they ran to Mark's house.
Danny threw the present
into the skip.

'That was fun!' he said.
'Let's dump some more!'

Mark and Danny
dumped more of
Granny's stupid presents.

Then Mark ran off home.

Danny smiled to himself.
Santa will be pleased,
he thought.

There's lots of room
under my tree.
I have lots of food
for Rudolph.
And Granny might help me
clean the chimney.

Danny bent down beside
Granny's chair.
He looked up the chimney.
It was dark and dusty.

'Granny,' he shouted.
'Will you help me
clean the chimney?'

But Granny just snored.

'Nnnnn – HAAAAAAAAAAAAA.

Nnnnn – HAAAAAAAAAAAAA.'

Danny called Mum.
'Will you help me
clean the chimney?'
he yelled.

Mum was too busy.
'I'm looking for
the roasting tin,' she said.
'I can't find it anywhere.'

Danny shook his head.
I'll have to clean
the chimney all by myself,
he thought.

Danny got the big garden hose.
He wheeled it into
the sitting room.
This will go all the way
up the chimney, he thought.

Then he went outside again
and turned on the garden tap.

The water gushed into the hose.

It gushed all the way
down the hose.

Danny ran back
to the sitting room.

And the water
gushed out.

But it didn't go up the chimney.
It gushed all over Granny.
She jumped up.
She waved her arms.
She coughed and spluttered.

She was **soaked**.

Danny tried to grab the hose.
Granny tried to grab it too.

The hose jumped and
hopped around the room.
Granny jumped and
hopped too.

The hose knocked Granny
to the floor.

Then it hit the Christmas tree.
All the lights went out
and the tree came
crashing down.

Mum and Dad rushed in.

Danny dived behind the couch.

Mum picked up Granny.

Dad picked up

the Christmas tree.

Danny sneaked upstairs.

Next morning,
Danny woke very early.
It was snowing.
'It's Christmas!' he yelled.

He dashed downstairs.

'Happy Christmas, Danny,'
said Mum.
She was putting towels
on the floor.

'I think Santa has left something for you,' said Dad. He was putting new bulbs in the Christmas-tree lights.

Danny saw a huge box
under the tree.
He dived in.

Danny tore open the box.
'**Yesssssss**!' he sang.
He jumped up and down
with joy.

'The HD Mega Game-Station 4!' he screamed.

'I hope Santa gave me some **games** too!'

Danny searched the box.
He couldn't see any games.

He punched the box.
'What good is the HD Mega
Game-Station 4
without games?' he moaned.

But Granny said:
'Santa can't bring everything.
He's very busy. That's why
he asks **grannies**
to help!'

And Granny began
to crawl under the tree.

Danny clapped his hands.
He hugged his HD Mega
Game-Station 4.

'Oh Granny!' he said.
'You got me some games!
You're the **BEST**!'

Granny pulled presents.
She pushed presents.
She squeezed presents.
Then she shook her head.

'I had four wonderful games
for you, Danny,' she said.
'I had them wrapped
in fancy paper and a
big blue ribbon.'

'But I can't find them anywhere,' said Granny.

Danny dropped his HD Mega Game-Station 4 with a bang. '**A big blue ribbon**! **NO**!'

Danny raced out the front door.
The snow was very deep.
'The skip! The skip!' he yelled.

But the skip was **gone**.

Danny was very cross.
He stamped his foot.
It landed in Mum's roasting tin.
'Aaaaaaaaaaaaagh!' he cried.
He slid down the path
in the snow.

Everyone laughed.

But Danny didn't laugh.
'I'll never do anything
like this again,' he said.
'NEVER. NEVER. NEVER.'

But I think he will, don't you?
Danny's just that kind of kid.